GLAZED AND ACCUSED

RAISED AND GLAZED COZY MYSTERIES, BOOK 41

EMMA AINSLEY

SUMMER PRESCOTT BOOKS PUBLISHING

CHAPTER ONE

Maggie Mission woke early on her day off. She dressed while Brett, her husband and former county sheriff, readied himself for work at the satellite location for their Dogwood Mountain donut shop.

"Everyone is entitled to a day off," he reminded her before he left. "You never worried about it when I was still sheriff."

"But that was before you took on the same job I have," Maggie argued with him. "I feel really guilty having a day to myself while you're stuck behind the counter."

"You never have an opinion when Bradley takes a day off at his donut shop in Hunter Springs."

"That's because Bradley is my son," Maggie said. "He's also a father and husband with a small family. I'm a middle-aged woman with all the time in the world on my hands."

"If that was true, you wouldn't need a day off from work," Brett said. He kissed her lightly on the forehead before he headed out into the dark morning.

Maggie stifled her twinge of guilt and got ready for a day out of the house. She wore her favorite jeans and a light sweater, a change from her typical work uniform at the donut shop, and headed toward the lake for one of the final days of the farmer's market. She had missed many early mornings at the market during the summer and early fall when work kept her busy. But today she intended to browse around the farm stands and take her time selecting fresh fruits and vegetables.

The parking lot at the lake was already full when she arrived. It was just before eight in the morning and the market was packed. Maggie parked her car and gathered her canvas shopping bags together on her arm, determined to fill every square inch of them with goodies before she headed back home for the day. She planned to look for a mincemeat pie for Orson, her favorite customer and former employee. Orson mentioned his favorite pie from time to time and Maggie was determined to find one for him.

A chilly breeze greeted her when she opened her car door. Maggie figured the chill in the air may have been thanks to the lake, but she grabbed a hooded sweatshirt from the backseat before she headed through the front entrance to the market and began looking around.

She passed several vendors before she stopped to make her first purchase. A pair of Mennonite women stood behind a small folding table laden with fresh pies, breads, donuts, and other goodies. Maggie smiled when she spotted the only mincemeat pie on the table. She made her selection and paid for her purchase, gladly gifting the younger of the two women a tip for her remarkable looking creation.

Maggie's feet felt light as she glided through the next few booths. She could hardly wait to see the look on Orson's face when she presented him with the pie. As the self-appointed father figure of Maggie and her closest friends, he maintained a sour expression at all times just to impart his displeasure on any scheme he deemed silly or dangerous or simply ill-advised.

When she was about halfway through the first group of vendors, Maggie stopped to admire a wicker basket filled to the brim with the brightest strawberries she had ever seen. The vendor, an older woman named Lois whom Maggie had met before, waved her hand over the strawberries. "Take all of them if you want," she said. "I'll make you a deal. I can't look at another strawberry after this year's bumper crop."

"But you could preserve them," Maggie said, admiring the rows of jams and jellies displayed on the other side of the woman's booth.

"Don't you even suggest it," Lois said. "I have jammed and jellied and frozen and even dehydrated more strawberries this year than I've seen in all my seventy-two years on this planet. If I never smell the aroma of cooked strawberries again, it will be too soon."

Maggie laughed and negotiated a deal for three five-gallon buckets filled with the fruit. She had already planned out how to use the bounty at the donut shop. Lois directed her grandson, a strapping young man of about nineteen, to help load the buckets into Maggie's car. Maggie thanked the young man and insisted he take her tip before she headed back into the market to finish her shopping, which she was in no great hurry to do.

"I have to ask you," a woman approached her and said as she made her way past the Mennonite women for the second time. The woman stood several inches taller than Maggie and was dressed in flowing, colorful layers. Another woman stood right behind her and frowned as the first woman spoke. "Are you some sort of farm wife or something?"

"Pardon me," Maggie said, not sure she appreciated the odd question from a perfect stranger.

"I'm serious," the woman said. "I just saw you hefting those buckets of strawberries to your car. What are you going to do, preserve it all? Make some sort of strawberry wine out of it? I just can't help myself from asking."

"No, as a matter of fact," Maggie said, still slightly offended. "I own a chain of donut shops in the area, and I plan to incorporate fresh strawberries into a featured variety this week."

"Donuts? That's weird," the woman said. She ran her hand through her short hair and glared at Maggie.

"What she means to say is how interesting," the shorter woman interjected. Unlike her companion, she was dressed in normal clothes. Her blond hair hung almost to her waist. "I'm Angel Harris and this is Dessi Shroyer. We're both business owners and saw you carrying the strawberries out and wondered what they were for. That's all."

"Maggie Mission," she said cautiously. "Pleased to meet you."

"Yeah, yeah," Dessi said, interrupting their conversation. "So, tell me about this donut. How on earth are you going to use fresh fruit with a deep-fried donut? Seems like such a waste to me. As a matter of fact, that sounds like something that ought to be illegal, like mixing patterns or wearing socks with sandals at the beach."

"I think I would like to continue shopping," Maggie said. "If you will excuse me."

"Of course," Angel said, stepping out of the way.

"Geez, what flew into her bonnet and spoiled the day," Maggie heard Dessi remark as she walked away. She rolled her eyes and headed for the other side of the farmer's market, eager to avoid the odd pair.

After she left the lake, Maggie drove directly to the donut shop to drop off the buckets. She entered through the back door with one of the buckets in her arms.

"What on earth?" Myra Sawyer-Macklin exclaimed. "Where have you been?"

"The farmer's market," Maggie replied. She gestured to the cooler door. "Can you open that for me?"

"Of course," Myra said, rushing to get the door for her boss. "What is that?"

"Fresh strawberries," Maggie replied as she wiped the perspiration from her brow. "There are two more buckets out in the car."

"I'll help," Naomi Gardner, another employee and close friend of Maggie's, said. Maggie followed her outside to the alley behind the donut shop and they removed the final two buckets. "Are you planning to make something new?"

"I wasn't until I saw these at the farmers market," Maggie said. "I thought about trying a new recipe."

"What are you thinking?" Naomi asked her as they walked back inside the shop.

"Maybe an angel food donut with a strawberry compote."

"That's ironic," Ruby said, joining them. Ruby Cobb was Maggie's best friend and business partner, and a decorated former executive chef with a string of best-selling cookbooks to her credit. "I was just experimenting with a new angel food donut recipe last night."

"Could you use these strawberries?" Maggie asked.

"You better believe it," Ruby said, taking the last bucket from her. She hefted the large bucket onto the prep table and cracked open the lid. "Oh, they smell perfect."

"For Pete's sake," Orson grumbled from his normal perch atop a wooden stool next to the baker's table. "Don't tell me you can smell how good a strawberry is now."

"As a matter of fact, I can," Ruby said. She turned to wink at Naomi and Maggie. "It's just a little trick I learned in culinary school."

"Oh, pish posh," Orson said, waving his hand in the air in her direction. "Now I've heard everything."

"I have something for you." Maggie beamed. "Be right back." She turned and headed straight back out to the car, plucking the mincemeat pie out of one of her cloth shopping bags. She carried it carefully through the door.

"What is this?" Orson asked when she held up the pie.

"Only a homemade mincemeat pie," Maggie said, stretching her arms out to him. "Fresh baked this morning."

"Mincemeat pie," Orson said. His eyes widened as he took the pie from her. "Where on earth did you get this?"

"At the farmers market." Maggie smiled. "From the Mennonite ladies. It was the last one on the table."

"How much do I owe you?" Orson said, not taking his eyes off of the pie.

"It's a gift," Maggie said softly.

"A gift? For me?" Orson repeated, as if he couldn't believe his ears.

"Just do me a favor," Ruby said. "When you go out to the Old Timer's table in the front, please make sure everyone understands that we are not selling mince-meat pies now."

"Who says I'm going to eat it here?" Orson asked, bringing it close to his body.

"Would you like me to cut a wedge of it for you?" Myra stepped forward to ask. "We can put the rest of it in the cooler."

"Actually, yes," Orson said, nodding. "I wouldn't mind having a piece right now."

"How about some coffee to go with it?" Maggie offered.

"That sounds perfect," Orson said, blinking back his emotions. "Sometimes you girls are too good to me."

Maggie exchanged a knowing glance with Ruby and headed to the front for a fresh cup of coffee. As she was pouring his cup, Orson walked solemnly through the swinging kitchen door and to the Old Timer's table on the far side of the dining area. Maggie followed him with the mug and sat it down in front of him.

"This is so good," he said as he took his first bite.

"I'm glad it's good," Maggie said, still beaming. She placed her hand affectionately on his shoulder and looked outside. Despite the chilly morning, the sun had warmed up the day considerably. She scanned the parking lot, taking note of her small donut truck parked close to the road. She spotted something in the church parking lot across the street and walked outside the front door.

"What is it?" Orson asked, following her outside.

"It looks like another food truck," Maggie said. "I'm surprised the church let them park there."

"Maybe they saw yours and decided it was okay," Orson suggested.

"Maybe," Maggie said. "But the food truck in our parking lot matches the sign above it."

"I'm just sorry to see it's not Flo back here with her truck," Orson mused. "I sure wish she was back here again."

Maggie recalled another food truck aptly named The Diner, which had parked for many months beneath the sign close to her own mobile donut shop. "She's very happy at her new, permanent location," Maggie said, although she wished the same. Flo's food was fantastic, as was her friendship.

"Well, maybe that's what these people are hoping for," Orson suggested, nodding to the brightly colored truck. It was parked close to the edge of the parking lot next to an empty field.

Maggie shrugged and headed back inside. Orson followed her, eager to return to his wedge of mincemeat pie.

She decided to take advantage of the rest of her day off as she walked through the kitchen toward the back door. "Ruby, what do you know about that food truck across the road?" she asked as she picked up her things.

"I just noticed that this morning," Ruby said. "I wonder how the church feels about it."

"That's what I was wondering, too," Maggie said. She shrugged. "Maybe they hope to buy that land next to the church. It's for sale, after all."

"That land has been for sale since I started working here," Naomi said. "Maybe they found a buyer at last."

"It does seem like an odd place to park a food truck," Ruby said. "I guess they're hoping to get some over-flow from our customer base."

"Yeah, considering how close to the edge of town we are here," Myra added.

Maggie shrugged again and headed out the door. She still had a back seat full of groceries from the farmer's market to unload and a movie to catch up on before her return to work the next day.

CHAPTER TWO

"You have to try this," Ruby said when Maggie walked into the kitchen the following morning. It was before five o'clock, and Maggie was struggling to wake up.

"What is it?" Maggie asked, glaring at the plate Ruby held in front of her face. "It looks like a donut."

"Not just any donut," Ruby said. Maggie glanced around the kitchen and noticed a large bowl of eggs for the first time on the prep table. "This is the angel food doughnut I was trying out at home. I made a fruit compote to go with it. You have to try this."

Maggie followed Ruby back to the commercial range where a large pan of stewed strawberries was cooling.

She waited as Ruby ladled a small amount of the fruit mixture onto the donut and topped it with a dollop of whipped cream.

While Ruby watched, Maggie cut a piece of the donut and swirled it around in the fruit mixture, then took a bite. Her eyes opened immediately, and she nodded her head. "Oh, my goodness," she said. "The fruit just explodes in your mouth. That donut is so good. What's different this time?"

"Well, for one thing, I used the freshest eggs I could find," Ruby said. "I made a quick trip to the farmer's market myself yesterday. In addition, I used real buttermilk and sour cream in the donut."

"Whatever you did, it makes a real difference," Maggie said, taking another bite. She carried the plate back to the office where she set her things down on the desk. "Did you use all of the strawberries?"

"Unfortunately, yes," Ruby said. "But I think we have a good template for the fruit compote from now on. I added the donut to the menu this morning. We have enough for a couple of days, I think."

"We need to add fresh strawberries to our next food order," Maggie said. She finished the donut off and didn't argue when Ruby added another to her plate. "Orson is going to go crazy over this."

"If Orson makes it in today." Ruby chuckled.

"Why wouldn't he?" Maggie asked, suddenly concerned.

"Go in the cooler and tell me what you see."

Not a fan of riddles, Maggie bit her bottom lip to prevent arguing with her best friend and headed to the cooler. She walked in and noticed the mincemeat pie still on the shelf. Only a single piece remained. "Did he eat this, or did he share it?" she asked as she emerged from the cooler.

"He ate it." Ruby nodded. "Every last piece, save the one that's in there. He went home not feeling too good last night."

"Oh, no," Maggie said, smiling despite herself. She pressed her palm to her forehead and shook her head. "I should never have given him the entire pie."

"The man is an adult," Ruby reminded her. "He's fully in charge of what he puts in his own body. The fact that he got a stomachache from eating too much mincemeat is not your fault."

"I'm surprised he didn't polish it off."

"I think he'd finally had enough. When he left here, he said he would never touch it again."

"We both know that's not true," Maggie said. She returned to the office and removed one of her favorite aprons from the small stack inside the door. She tied the apron around her back and immediately headed to the storage room for her supplies. Another cool morning prompted her to double the normal amount of cinnamon rolls she prepared. She also intended to return to a Dogwood Donuts classic favorite, apple cider donuts.

Ruby and Maggie worked non-stop until around nine o'clock when Ruby suggested taking a break together. Orson had still not made an appearance, though Maggie felt a little relief after speaking with Myra. Orson was at home in front of the TV, recovering from his stomachache.

Shortly after her engagement to then Officer Brooks Macklin, Myra found an old two-story home on the other side of town. After their wedding, Brooks and Myra invited Orson to come live with them in the in-law suite. Orson had accepted their invitation and made his home with the Macklin family, welcoming their daughter Lexi when she was born. Maggie was grateful to know someone always had an eye on Orson, even though in his mind he was the one keeping tabs on everyone else.

"I'm thinking I'm ready for one of those apple cider donuts," Ruby announced as she removed her apron and headed to the usual booth near the bathrooms on the far side of the counter.

"I think I'm with you," Maggie said. "Not that the angel food donuts aren't wonderful, I've just had my fill of them this morning."

"You don't want to fill up on them like Orson did on his pie yesterday," Ruby said, gently teasing her.

"Not on your life," Maggie said. She filled two mugs with coffee and headed to the booth. Ruby followed her with their donut selections. They settled in and began chatting easily together. Maggie listened as Ruby described the latest antics when she fed her small herd of cattle on her farm that morning. Maggie discussed the possibility that Suzan, her daughter-in-law, might be pregnant, though she wasn't sure how her grandson Wyatt might feel about another sibling.

A short time later, a new rush of customers sent Ruby back to the front for a moment to assist Naomi. She returned to the booth with a fresh refill of coffee. "I'm not ready to go back just yet," she whispered when she sat back down.

"Neither am I," Maggie said. "Which is terrible because I had a day off yesterday."

"What are you doing here?" a voice called above them. Maggie looked up and spotted the same color-fully-clad woman she had seen at the farmer's market the day before. "We met yesterday. I'm Dessi. Dessi Shroyer, remember? I think you said your name was Maggie. Is this your donut shop?"

When the woman finally stopped for a breath of air, Maggie pointed to Ruby. "This is my best friend and business partner, Ruby Cobb," she said. "Dessi and her business partner Angel were at the farmer's market yesterday."

"Yeah, well, Angel is running the show this morning," Dessi said dismissively. "I just wanted to stop by and check out the competition."

"Did you open a donut shop here in town?" Ruby asked, looking up at the taller woman.

"Not on your life," Dessi said, curling her top lip. "No, we run the food truck across the street. Sweet Stacks."

"So, you sell pancakes?" Maggie asked.

"Not pancakes," Dessi said, rolling her eyes. Maggie suddenly felt as if she had guessed wrong on a test at school. The woman had a way of making her feel about two inches tall. "No, we are a gourmet waffle truck. Hence the name, Sweet Stacks."

"I guess it would work either way," Ruby said. Maggie could tell she fought against her better nature to prevent herself from rolling her eyes.

"No, it wouldn't work," Dessi insisted. "In no way is Sweet Stacks an appropriate name for a pancake truck. What are you thinking?"

"Did you just come over to check things out?" Maggie asked brightly. She was eager not to allow the woman to insult Ruby.

"Yeah, it's something like that," Dessi said. She headed straight for the glass display case and planted both of her hands on top. Maggie cringed at the thought of the woman's handprints remaining behind. She cringed twice as hard when the woman pressed her face into the glass. "What did you do with the strawberries?"

"What are you doing?" Myra asked, emerging suddenly through the swinging door from the kitchen. "Please don't put your face on the glass."

"What's your problem?" Dessi asked when she stood upright. "I just wanted to see what was in there."

"You can see just fine from a respectable distance," Ruby said.

"Jeez Louise," Dessi said, rolling her eyes. "You people really need to get out more."

"To answer your question," Maggie said quickly. "We used the strawberries in a fruit compote with an angel food donut. Unfortunately, we have sold out already today."

"Hey, nobody said anything about me wanting to try one of your donuts," Dessi said, curling her top lip again.

"What can we do for you?" Ruby asked. "Would you like a cup of coffee? To go?" Maggie nearly choked when Ruby emphasized the request.

"Yeah. I think maybe I will," Dessi said. She narrowed her eyes at Ruby. "It's on the house, right? I would assume so after the rude way you've spoken to me this morning."

"Look," Maggie said, lowering her voice. "No one meant to insult you, but you have come on a little strong."

"That doesn't mean anything." Dessi laughed. "I'm a customer. And the customer is always right, or haven't you been in business very long?"

"We've been in business for several years," Ruby said.

"And who are you?" Dessi asked.

"She happens to be a best-selling cookbook author and a trained chef," Myra said. She pushed the cup of coffee across the counter to Dessi.

"Yeah, right," Dessi said, rolling her eyes. "You sure don't look like either of those things."

"What do I look like then?" Ruby asked, folding her arms over her chest.

"Hey, calm down," Dessi said. She sipped the coffee in her hand. "At least you can make good coffee, I suppose."

"Were you thinking about paying for that?" Ruby asked.

"I thought this was on the house," Dessi said. She walked towards the front door, opened the trash can and dropped the full cup of coffee inside. "It wasn't that good anyway."

Ruby, Myra, and Maggie watched the woman leave. She walked back across the parking lot and headed across the road.

"Well, that was pleasant," Ruby said, breaking the silence at last.

"I can think of another word for it," Maggie said.

"Let's hope she doesn't decide to keep her food truck parked across the street for very long," Myra added.

"Did you say there was another one of them?" Ruby asked. "A business partner or something?"

"Yeah, her name is Angel," Maggie said. "And she is much saner than her friend."

CHAPTER THREE

Orson made his way to the donut shop just before noon. He slumped into his chair at the Old Timer's table and rested his head on his hands.

"Would you like some coffee?" Maggie called to him from behind the counter.

"Yes, please," he replied, sounding weak and forlorn.

Myra emerged from the back with another tray of apple cider donuts for the display case. "It's about time you rolled in here, sleepyhead."

"Good morning to you, too."

"Maggie has your coffee," Myra said. "Would you like something for breakfast? Maybe a donut from the case or the last piece of that mincemeat pie?"

"Girl, don't you ever mention that pie in my presence again," Orson moaned.

"Have you sworn it off forever, then?" Maggie asked as she placed the coffee mug in front of him.

"Not forever," Orson said. "Just until the memory of my recent overindulgence is gone."

"Okay, then do you want anything to eat?" Myra asked.

"Maybe just some apple slaw if Ruby has any ready in the back," Orson said. Without another word, Maggie headed through the swinging door into the kitchen. Ruby met her just inside the door with a bowl of fresh apple slaw.

"I guess you heard his request," Maggie said.

"I heard." Ruby smiled. "I was watching him. He doesn't look very good, does he?"

"He has looked better," Maggie said. "Do you have enough of this made in case he wants more?"

"I'll make sure Orson has everything he needs," Ruby reassured her. Maggie headed back to the front with the apple slaw. She was shocked to see Angel enter the donut shop. After the interaction with Dessi, Maggie had hoped she had heard the last of the ladies from Sweet Stacks.

"Good morning," Maggie called to her as she approached the counter.

"I think it might be afternoon," Angel said.

"I think you're right." Maggie chuckled. She glanced at the time display on the tablet that served as a register at the front counter. "What can I do for you?"

"Maybe you can make a vanilla latte for me, for starters," Angel said. "I get quite sick of my own coffee."

"Alright," Maggie said. "One vanilla latte coming right up."

"Thanks," Angel said. Maggie was pleased to see her reach for her bank card. "What do I owe you?"

"Four dollars and fifty cents." Maggie smiled. Angel swiped her card through the reader and waited for the transaction to process.

"Can I get you anything else?"

"I do have a question for you," Angel said. "Have you seen my partner this morning? She was supposed to help me with the food truck all day. We still have a few things to do before we can actually open."

"You're not already opened?" Maggie asked.

"No. Not yet," Angel said. "This is a brand-new venture for both of us. Anyway, have you seen Dessi?"

"She was in here around nine, or a little after," Maggie said.

"And did she say much?" Angel asked.

"Nothing pleasant," Ruby said, walking behind Maggie.

"That sounds like her," Angel said with a slight laugh. "Was she angry or acting strange?"

"No, just unpleasant," Maggie said, shrugging slightly. "I don't mean to speak ill of her behind her back, but she wasn't very nice."

"Did you tell her about Dessi tossing a full cup of coffee she didn't pay for in the trash can by the front door?" Myra asked. She knelt in front of the display case to remove empty trays.

"I wasn't going to mention it," Maggie said with a grimace.

"It's alright," Angel said. "I'm getting used to it."

"Have you been partners for very long?" Maggie asked.

"Not very long at all," Angel said. She ran her hand through the front of her hair and stared at the wall behind the counter. "We just met in Tulsa last summer. My previous business partner abandoned me and Dessi was working for a competitor at the time. She was the one who convinced me to sell my brick and mortar store and invest in the food truck."

"What brought you to the Ozarks?" Maggie asked.

"Hope." Angel smiled. "To put it bluntly, we were hoping that we might find a better market for our waffles up here."

"Has that not turned out to be the case?" Maggie asked. She motioned to a nearby table and carried a mug of coffee with her. Angel sat down and sipped her latte.

"I thought things were going well," Angel said. "Then early this morning the pastor or whatever from the church came out shouting at us that we were parked there illegally."

"In the parking lot?" Maggie asked.

"Yes, right where you see the truck."

"Are you sure it was the pastor?" Maggie asked.

"I'm not sure of anything," Angel said. "Dessi is the one who has handled everything so far. She was supposed to have made a deal with the pastor to rent space in the parking lot while we worked out a deal with the owner of the lot for sale next to the church. I'm starting to think she was wrong about that. Either I'm confused, or she never spoke to the owner of the church at all."

"The man you spoke with was not the pastor," an elderly woman said from a few tables away. Maggie looked up and recognized her. She was a regular customer to the donut shop, a woman named Jean.

"Pardon me," Angel said, staring at her. "How do you know that?"

"Because I'm married to the pastor, and he's out of town at the moment," Jean said. "The man who talked to you is named Rick Holcomb, and he's the head of the deacons. He manages the facility, which is owned by the congregation and not the pastor."

"Jean, do you know what might be going on then?" Maggie asked the older woman gently. "It sounds as if there may have been some miscommunication at work here."

"I'm afraid there was no miscommunication, my dear," Jean said sadly. "As a matter of fact, there was no communication at all. The food truck simply showed up in the parking lot a few days ago. The deacons have been trying to talk to the owner about it since it arrived."

"But I am the owner," Angel said. Her tone was not abrasive or angry. She appeared confused.

"That may be," Jean said simply. "But the other woman is the one who has been forcing herself on the church. It was just this morning that the deacons met and decided to deal with it. The next step is calling the police in to handle things."

"I don't understand any of this," Angel said. She stood up suddenly, almost spilling her latte on the table. "I have to go."

"Angel," Maggie said, standing up. "Slow down. Maybe you should reach out to the deacons yourself and even the property owner. It sounds like the miscommunication has happened between you and Dessi."

"I highly doubt your friend has been in touch with a property owner," Jean continued.

"Why do you say that?" Maggie asked.

"Because Timothy DeBell owns that property," Jean said. "And he's been stuck in a nursing home in Joplin for the past eight months."

"Wait a minute," Angel said, shaking her head. "Are you telling me the property owner is actually a man named Timothy?"

"It sounds like you were told something different," Maggie said.

"Yeah, you could say that," Angel said. She headed for the door.

"Hold on a minute," Maggie said, walking after her. "Who did you think owned the property?"

"Dessi told me it was some woman named Margaret Chase," Angel said. "She told me Margaret worked as a real estate agent here in town and wanted to sell the property as soon as possible."

"Oh, no," Jean said, shaking her head. "And I've never heard of a real estate agent by that name anywhere in this area."

"I can't believe this," Angel said. She paused at the door for a moment, then headed out into the parking lot.

"I don't know whether I should feel sorry for her or angry," Jean said, shaking her head.

"If what she says is true," Orson spoke up from his seat, "I would feel nothing but sorry for that girl."

"Yeah," Maggie said, staring after Angel as she made her way back across the road to the church parking lot. "It sounds like she just got taken for a ride." She headed back to the kitchen with her coffee.

"What was that all about?" Ruby asked.

"I guess Dessi and Angel have some issues in their business partnership," Maggie said. "The pastor's wife, Jean, happened to be here and informed her that everything Dessi has been telling her is false."

"Where is Angel now?" Ruby asked.

"I guess she went back across the street to see if Dessi was at the food truck," Maggie said as she got back to work. "That's why she came here in the first place."

"Hey, Maggie," Myra said, appearing in the doorway about an hour later. "Brooks is out here and wants to speak with you."

"Myra, if your husband is out front, you know you can send him back here to the kitchen," Ruby said.

"Well, he says that it's official business."

Maggie shivered slightly. "Even so," she said, smiling despite the slight feeling of dread that crept up her spine. "Send him back here. Official business is all the more reason for him to speak to us in private."

Myra turned around for a moment, then moved out of the way to let Brooks through.

"Maggie," Brooks said. His face was drawn and serious. "Can we talk in the office?"

"Yeah, sure," Maggie said. She glanced wearily at Ruby and headed back to the far corner of the kitchen. She held open the door for Brooks and took a seat behind her desk. "What's going on?"

"Myra just filled me in on Angel Harris' visit here a little while ago," Brooks began.

"What about it?"

"Was she looking for Dessi Shroyer?" Brooks asked.

"Yes, that's why she stopped in," Maggie said. "What's going on?"

"We found a vehicle parked at the lake a little while ago," Brooks said. "It was just inside the city limits, which is why I'm here and not the sheriff."

"Okay…"

"A woman's body was inside the vehicle," Brooks said slowly. "She was in the back seat. Her face was blue, and we found a plastic bag around her neck. She was murdered."

"Have you identified her?" Maggie asked tremulously.

"I think you already know what I'm going to say."

"It was Dessi Shroyer, wasn't it?" Maggie's mouth suddenly went dry.

"Yes, it was," Brooks said. "We found identification on her, and a former business partner has stepped forward to identify her."

"That seems fast," Maggie said. "Who is this business partner and where did they come from?"

"The former business partner had just arrived in town from the Tulsa area," Brooks said. "Her name is Yara Scott, and she claims to have been concerned about Dessi and Angel for some time."

CHAPTER FOUR

"Why didn't you tell me what was going on?" Brett asked Maggie later that night. He'd arrived home a short time after she'd left the donut shop, his eyes wild with concern.

"Everything just happened so fast," Maggie said. "That terrible woman showed up this morning and gave me a rough time at the donut shop. Then, her business partner showed up looking for her and an hour later Brooks was in the kitchen telling me Dessi had been found dead."

"You could have called me," Brett said.

"I actually assumed Brooks had already done that." Maggie shrugged. She was in no mood to argue with her husband. Her upper back and neck muscles were tied in knots from the stress of the day.

"Why would you assume that?" Brett said, taking a seat in the kitchen. "There's a reason he came to see you."

"He explained that to me," Maggie said. "Because both of those women had been into the donut shop in the past day or so."

"That's not all," Brett said darkly. "Maggie, this case has been turned over to the county sheriff's department, and I think it will be turned over to the state police before the end of the day."

"I wonder why?"

"Because Dessi Shroyer's family back in Tulsa is involved," Brett said. "I don't know what her family is into, but this has become a bi-state case."

"But she was found dead within the city limits of Dogwood Mountain," Maggie said. "Why would the state police be involved?"

"For the same reasons I just explained," Brett said. "Her family has involved the Oklahoma State police, and that tends to go beyond just a small-town police department."

"Why are you telling me all this?" Maggie asked. "I've already answered Brooks' questions. This case has nothing more to do with me."

"Maggie, you have been my wife long enough to know cases like this tend to evolve," Brett said. "Brooks couldn't say much when he visited you today but make no mistake. His visit was a courtesy call."

"I'm still not following," Maggie said, slowly shaking her head.

"Like it or not, your recent interactions with both of those women puts you on a short list of suspects," Brett said. "You, and maybe Ruby, too. The fact that some negative words were exchanged between you and the victim is not a good thing, Maggie."

"Hold on a minute," she said. "You're saying I'm a suspect? How could I be a suspect? I don't even know what the woman drove."

"Right, but the Missouri State police don't know you from Adam," Brett said. "It's not like having Brooks investigate something. It's not even like having the sheriff investigate something. They don't know you.

They don't know that you had nothing to do with this woman's death."

"There's no evidence to suggest otherwise," Maggie said. "Is there something else going on that I don't know about?"

"All I'm saying is that you're already on a list of people the state police are looking at," Brett said. "As soon as word got out that Dessi's body had been found in her car, plenty of people called the sheriff's department to report the exchange between Ruby, you, and Dessi at the donut shop. A few more people called and said they had seen you talking to both women at the farmers market the other day. Is this starting to become a little more clear you?"

"The only thing that isn't clear is why you seem to be angry at me for something," Maggie said. "What have I done?"

Brett rested his head in his hands. He exhaled slowly. "I'm sorry," he said at last. "You're right. I'm taking this out on you. Clearly this isn't your fault. I'm just worried."

"But why are you so worried?" Maggie asked. She took the seat next to his and rested her hand on his shoulder. "I had nothing to do with this, neither did Ruby. Neither of us were anywhere near Dessi or the park by the lake. Why would you think we have something to worry about?"

"I suppose it's because of the visitor I had myself this morning," Brett said. "You wouldn't remember him, but there was a rookie deputy that served under me when I was sheriff, just about the same time you came back to Dogwood Mountain. Anyway, he's moved on and moved up in the Missouri State Police ranks. He stopped in at the donut shop to catch up with me and informed me that he was in town to investigate Dessi's disappearance. He said someone had given him the tip that he should look into the lady who runs the donut shop in town."

"I don't like the sound of that," Maggie said. "But you already told me plenty of people had seen our exchange of words and called in. Why does this particular trooper worry you?"

"First of all, he's not just a state trooper," Brett said. "He's worked himself up to captain. Captain Andrew Flint. I don't like the fact that he already knew about the woman running the donut shop. It almost sounds like someone's trying to frame you for this."

"Frame me? For what reason?" Maggie said. Her voice rose sharply. "I have nothing to do with these people. I just met them at the farmers market on my day off. I didn't ask them to approach me. Why would I be someone's target?"

"I'm not sure," Brett said. He rose from his seat and stared out the kitchen window. "But my gut instinct tells me something is off here. Something is way off."

"And now I'm worried," Maggie said. She flapped her arms at her side and stormed off to the bedroom on the far end of the house.

"Maggie," Brett called after her. "I wasn't trying to make you worried."

"Too late," she called through the closed bedroom door.

"I just want you to be aware," Brett said.

Maggie pulled the door open and stood in the doorway. "You want me to be aware of what, exactly?" she asked. "Aware that someone may or may not be trying to frame me for the murder of someone I just met? Right. What's to worry about?"

"I really messed this one up, didn't I?" Brett leaned against the door frame. "I don't mean to scare you. I just want you to be aware of what's going on around you. I know we don't have anything to worry about, and that you had nothing to do with this. But the circumstances all jumbled together really concern me."

"Maggie."

"No," she said. "I'm going to see Ruby. I'll be back later."

On her way to Ruby's farm, Maggie did her best not to overthink. She wanted to talk things out with her friend.

"So, let me get this straight," Ruby said when they were seated near the fire pit. "I get that Dessi was found dead, but what about the guy Brett knows? He's part of the state highway patrol?"

"But he's not a trooper," Maggie said, mocking Brett's voice. "This Captain Flint served under Brett back when he was sheriff. Supposedly, he stopped by to check out the donut shop because there was a tip that a person of interest was the lady at the donut shop."

"Was that the actual tip?"

"According to Brett it was," Maggie said. "Only, it sounds as if that was hours before Brooks came to visit me."

"But how would he have known about it already?" Ruby asked.

"That's what I'm wondering."

"It was afternoon when Angel stopped by the donut shop to ask about Dessi."

"Which means she hadn't seen Dessi for several hours," Maggie said. "In fact, she told me she hadn't seen her at all that morning."

"I don't get any of this," Ruby said. She sat back in her chair and stared at the sky overhead. "How did these people even get involved in our lives?"

"Apparently because I bought too many strawberries at the farmers market."

"Well, that makes perfect sense." Ruby frowned.

"That's the whole reason Dessi and Angel approached me in the first place," Maggie explained. "Dessi came at me with some snide remark about being a farm wife or something, wondering why I was buying so many strawberries."

"That's why she approached you?"

"Angel was apologetic after Dessi's remarks," Maggie said quietly. "Why do I get the strong feeling Dessi knew how to make people upset at her?"

"Because you're more than likely right," Ruby said. "She sounds like a real gem."

"Only now she's dead. Oh, how did I get involved in this?" Maggie groaned.

"You mean how did we get involved in this? According to Brett, I might be on that short list of suspects, too."

"It's funny, isn't it?" Maggie asked suddenly. "I've yet to be officially questioned by anyone, including Brooks."

"That doesn't mean anything."

"Maybe not," Maggie said. "But it sure feels like somebody's trying awfully hard to point them in our direction."

"I get that same feeling," Ruby said. "The timeline for this is so short."

Maggie nodded. "Okay, so, let's concentrate on the timeline. I met them yesterday on my day off while I was at the farmer's market."

"Then Dessi showed up around nine," Ruby said. "And of course, she had to start insulting everyone in sight."

"Right, and then Angel showed up around noon to ask if we'd seen Dessi. But in all that time, someone from Tulsa contacted the police concerned about Dessi, and someone else had time to call a tip into the state police? None of this makes sense."

"I know," Ruby agreed. "I'm completely stumped. Less than three hours passed between Dessi showing up at the donut shop and Angel stopping by to ask if we had seen her."

"We can't forget about the deacon or whoever from the church," Maggie said. "At some point this morning, he stopped by and read Angel the riot act for being there."

"Are you adding him to the list of suspects?"

"To my list of suspects…" Maggie smiled. "Maybe. Although we don't know what time he talked to Angel."

"I have questions about this other woman, the one from Oklahoma," Ruby said. "How did she know Dessi was missing? Even if she showed up here from Tulsa this morning to talk to her, everything seems to have happened so fast."

"We know what caused her death," Maggie said. She stared out at the field for a moment to collect her thoughts. "We know Dessi was strangled in her car, and we know it happened sometime between nine this morning and well, whenever Brooks got the call to check out her car."

"We don't know that she was strangled in her car," Ruby said suddenly. "Maybe someone strangled her somewhere else and placed her in her car. We just don't have that information yet."

Maggie stood up and stretched her arms over her head. "None of this makes any sense," she said suddenly. "Usually when someone goes missing, there's a period of time where people try to look for them before they report them to the police."

"Unless they know something they're not sharing," Ruby suggested.

"Like what though?" Maggie asked. "We saw Dessi ourselves this morning. We know for a fact that she wasn't missing. How could someone from Tulsa realize their friend was missing and then drive all the way up here to investigate? It doesn't make a bit of sense to me."

"That's probably because we're missing a great deal of the story," Ruby said. "Hopefully the police realize that too."

CHAPTER FIVE

"Did you get that shipment of strawberries yet?" Orson asked Maggie the following morning.

"No. The truck hasn't been here yet."

Orson frowned and took a seat in front of the counter. He rested his elbows on the countertop and stared at the menu board in front of him. "I really wanted one of those angel food donuts with that strawberry sauce Ruby makes."

"If you want an angel food donut with the strawberry compote, all you have to do is ask. We have a few fresh strawberries in the back. We just haven't put out any of the donuts this morning because we don't have enough for the public."

"I'm not the public?" Orson asked.

"Oh, no," Maggie said, shaking her head. "You are something else entirely."

"For once, I'm not sure if I should be insulted or not."

"It's a compliment," Ruby said, reaching around Maggie. She set a platter on the counter in front of Orson. "There you are. I knew you'd be coming."

He said nothing, but his eyes devoured the contents of the platter before he took his first bite. Maggie glanced over her shoulder at Ruby, who winked then nodded toward the kitchen.

"You enjoy your angel food donuts," Maggie said. "Just don't advertise to everyone else what you have, okay?"

"No argument from me." He cut into the first donut, swirling the bite around in the still warm strawberry sauce.

"We really do spoil that man," Ruby said when Maggie joined her in the back.

"Of course we do." Maggie smiled. "And every one of us loves doing it."

"You got that right," Myra said as she passed them on the way to the swinging door. "I'll cover the front for now."

"Did you want to talk to me?" Maggie asked Ruby.

"I sure did," Ruby said. "When I ran to the bank just a little while ago, I took the long way back just so I could pass in front of the church across the street."

"I have a feeling you're about to tell me something juicy," Maggie said, leaning her weight against the baker's table.

"That food truck is surrounded by yellow police tape," Ruby said with a long sigh.

"What do you think that means?"

"I have absolutely no idea. I just wanted you to hear about it from me."

"Why do I get the feeling this murder investigation is creeping closer and closer to our front door?"

"It quite literally is," Ruby said. "It's taken every ounce of strength I have to refrain from grilling Myra over what she might know."

"Myra has never revealed anything to us she was asked not to by her husband."

"That's probably because Brooks never reveals anything he isn't supposed to." Ruby laughed.

"What should we do?" Maggie asked. "We have a vague idea that we might be suspects in this murder investigation, but no one has approached us yet. Do we just carry on with business as usual? Or maybe hit the pavement and ask questions on our own?"

"I think we just get through the workday, for now."

"And hope no one shows up to complicate our lives even further."

The swinging kitchen door opened and Orson wandered in, still holding his plate of angel food donuts in his hands. "Someone better start talking." He found his way to his normal stool next to the baker's table.

Maggie glanced at Ruby with a look that meant she did not want to discuss their troubles with the older man. "Start talking about what?"

"About what's going on around here," Orson said. "Don't you sit there and tell me there isn't something going on. I can read it in your faces."

"What exactly can you read?" Ruby asked.

"It started this morning," Orson said. "Myra and Brooks both buttoned their lips and didn't say a word to each other. That usually means something is going on."

"We have no idea what's going on between Brooks and Myra," Maggie said innocently. "Whatever is going on in their marriage is none of our business."

"Then I come here this morning and the two of you are watching the windows like hawks," Orson continued.

"What do you think we could possibly be looking for?"

"Don't play dumb, ladies." Orson finished the last bite and set the plate and fork on the table next to him. He folded his arms defiantly and pursed his lips awaiting Ruby's answer.

"This is silly," Ruby said. "We both have a lot of work to do. The truck is supposed to be here in less than an hour. You know how long that takes."

"Keep it up," Orson said. "Keep up your little charade of silence or whatever else is going on here. If I have to, I'll resort to calling Brett. Something is going on around here, and I have a right to know."

Ruby glanced at Maggie this time. "Brett is rather busy this morning himself. As soon as the truck leaves here, it heads straight to his store."

"I knew it," Orson said, jumping to his feet. He held his index finger just inches from Ruby's face. "Brett's in on it too, isn't he? There really is something big going on around here. And I bet it has something to do with that woman who was found dead in her car. Tell me I'm wrong."

"Okay, fine," Maggie said. She threw her arms up in exasperation. "We may as well tell him. He's just going to badger us until he figures it out."

"If you must know," Ruby said. "Brett has the concern that Maggie or I, or maybe both of us, might be on the state police radar as suspects in the woman's death."

"Oh, that's ridiculous," Orson said, batting his hand in the air. "Why on earth would they think the two of you had something to do with it?"

"Because a Captain Andrew Flint, a deputy once employed under Brett, showed up at the Jefferson Street location asking questions," Maggie explained. "The state police got a tip about Dessi Shroyer's death that indicated they needed to talk to the lady who runs the donut shop in town. He just happened to show up where Brett works instead of here."

"That's an odd coincidence," Orson said. "I'm not sure why it means you're a suspect, though."

"Think about it," Ruby said. "This was a very short time after Dessi was even found in her car. And someone had already mentioned the lady who runs the donut shop?"

"It just seems like someone is trying awfully hard to put us on the radar," Maggie said.

"Well, I guess I can see why that has everyone preoccupied," Orson said, nodding his head. "But it's utterly ridiculous that either of you would worry about it. Neither of you were anywhere near there yesterday. And what reason would you have for killing this woman? She was a complete stranger."

"We've both asked those same questions," Ruby admitted. "It doesn't mean we aren't worried."

"You can be worried," Orson said. "Just don't be silly."

"Maggie," Myra said, poking her head through the swinging door. "That lady is back, the one who's married to the pastor of the church across the street. She's out here talking about that food truck and the woman who died. I just thought I would let you know."

"That would be Jean," Maggie said. "She was here yesterday when Angel stopped by looking for Dessi."

"Do we need to do something about that?" Ruby asked.

"Of course you do," Orson said. "You need to get out there and listen in on what she has to say."

"You want one of us to go out there and eavesdrop?" Maggie asked.

"Absolutely." Orson nodded. "Go and listen to what she's telling everyone. You're bound to find out some more information from her flapping gums."

CHAPTER SIX

Maggie walked casually through the kitchen door. She stopped and began cleaning the counter. It took no time to overhear Jean discussing the food truck still parked in the church's parking lot.

"I got to the church at seven this morning," Jean was saying. She was surrounded by a group of ladies seated at her table. "That's when the cops first showed up."

"But I thought you said it wasn't the cops," one of the women said.

"I said it wasn't Dogwood Mountain cops," Jean said, craning her neck for emphasis. "It was the state police. I saw them just as sure as I'm sitting here.

They went through that food truck for an hour and a half before they wrapped it up in that ugly yellow tape. I just want to know what they were looking for."

"Probably for evidence," Orson muttered behind Maggie. She had not heard him join her behind the counter.

"I want to know if they found that other girl," Jean said. "You know, the one who was in here yesterday?"

"Is she missing, too?" one of her companions asked.

"I'm not sure, but I do know that poor old Rick Holcomb has been raked over the coals by the cops."

"What happened to Rick?" one of the women asked.

"According to Wanda, he was pulled in for questioning yesterday," Jean said. "They interviewed him at the police department, though I don't think it was our local guys doing the talking."

"What happened?" someone asked.

"What do you mean what happened?" Jean snapped. "They took him down to the police station and asked him a bunch of questions. What did you expect to happen?"

"I mean, did they arrest him or not?"

"How should I know?" Jean shrugged. "I just know what Wanda told me. I haven't heard any more from her. I called her five times this morning and she didn't pick up her phone."

"That could be because her husband's been arrested," Orson said a little too loudly.

"Rick Holcomb was arrested?" one of the women turned her attention from Jean to Orson. "Do you know that for sure?"

"I don't know anything about it," Orson said, taking his seat at the Old Timer's table. "I was just answering your question."

"Then why would you say that?" Jean huffed. "Unless you know something for sure, why would you say anything at all?"

"Maybe because you're all over here asking a ridiculous amount of questions," Orson said. "I was just suggesting one possible answer. Maybe this Rick guy was arrested."

"Did you hear he was arrested?" another woman asked.

"I haven't heard a thing," Orson said. "Aside from the cackling you hens are doing. All you're doing is sitting around speculating about things."

"Excuse me," Jean said. "Just who do you think you are?"

"As if you don't know." He shook his head and leaned back casually in his chair. "My name is Orson Hawley. My girls run this place, and that's all you need to know."

Maggie chewed on her lip to prevent herself from laughing out loud. She glanced in Orson's direction. His eyes locked with hers and revealed the fun he was having with the ladies at the table.

"What was that all about?" Ruby asked Maggie when she returned to the kitchen. "Did you find out anything new?"

"Nothing I didn't already know," Maggie said. "Like the fact that Orson loves to torment people who ask stupid and obvious questions."

"Do I want to know?" Ruby asked.

"No, you don't," Maggie said. "As far as the murder investigation goes, the only thing I learned is that

Rick Holcomb, the head deacon of the church, was questioned for several hours by the police. And that the state police showed up around seven this morning and searched the food truck for over an hour."

"You got all of that from that lady sitting out there?" Naomi said.

"Do you mean the pastor's wife?" Ruby asked. "It has been my experience that the wives of pastors tend to have the best tidbits of gossip to share."

"I'm sure that's not always the case," Maggie said. "But, in the case of Jean, it's very true."

After work, Maggie headed straight home for a shower. She was determined to present a good face to Brett when he returned home, rather than stoke more worry in him.

"How was your day?" Brett asked when he arrived at home shortly after three.

"Typical," Maggie said with a slight shrug. "Jean from the church was in the dining room speaking very loudly about the police investigating the Sweet Stacks food truck this morning."

"Did she say much? Were there any arrests?"

"Not that she indicated," Maggie said.

"Maybe she just didn't see it take place."

"No. I think she probably watched every bit of it. She's the kind to stand at her window and watch something take place from start to finish."

"What else did she say?" Brett asked.

"Something about the man who had confronted Angel about the food truck in the first place. Rick Holcomb, the head of the deacons at their church. I guess he was taken in for questioning and hasn't been heard from since."

"That's interesting."

"That's all you have to say? Yesterday you were all about the possibility of Ruby or me being in the crosshairs of law enforcement during this death investigation. Has something changed?"

"Not really," Brett said. "But I do find it interesting that no one has approached you yet. That makes me feel a little bit better about the entire situation."

"I'm starting to feel the same way," Maggie admitted. "Maybe the fact that Captain Flint showed up is simply insignificant."

"I wouldn't call it insignificant," Brett said. "The fact that someone mentioned the donut shop still has me concerned."

"Something else has puzzled me all day." Maggie wandered from the living room into the kitchen. "How would whoever came here from Tulsa even know to mention the donut shop?"

"They wouldn't," Brett said. "Not unless Angel herself tipped them off."

"That's where my line of thinking has gone, too."

"What are you thinking?"

"That maybe Angel had something to do with her death," Maggie admitted. "And maybe that's why she planted the idea of questioning the lady at the donut shop."

"It almost seems like that's the only explanation."

"I wonder where Angel is now?"

"I know," Brett agreed. "It's taking everything in me to keep from calling Brooks up and asking him for the low down."

"The low down? Listen to us," Maggie said, smiling. "We sound like a couple of bad TV scriptwriters."

"Yeah, well, at least we don't sound like we're panicked anymore."

"Do you actually think there's a reason to panic?"

"No, but I'm not completely convinced this investigation isn't going to come back on us," Brett said.

"I'm so sick of thinking about this," Maggie said suddenly. She clenched her fist next to her face and gritted her teeth. "I just want to get out of here for a little while."

"Like where?"

"I don't know," she said, opening her eyes. "Away?"

"I don't think we can break away from work right now."

"You're right," Maggie said, sinking into a chair at the kitchen table. "I just want to forget about food trucks and strangers and murder investigations."

"Let's go out to Ruby's," Brett suggested.

"And do what? Ruby is as concerned as I am about this."

"Okay, then let's go to Joplin for dinner," Brett suggested. "I'm sure no one there will be talking about Dessi Shroyer's death."

"That sounds good to me," Maggie said. She hopped up from the kitchen chair and headed straight to her bedroom.

"What are you doing?" he asked, following her in the room.

"Putting on something a little nicer," Maggie said. She slipped a sweater over her head and straightened her hair.

"Why don't we call Bradley and see if he wants to bring Suzan and the kids along?"

"That sounds like the perfect distraction."

CHAPTER SEVEN

Maggie slept soundly for the first time in a couple of days. There was something about spending time with her grandchildren, her son, and daughter-in-law that made her forget about the troubles in the world. She was disappointed to hear that the possibility of Suzan's pregnancy was a false alarm, but giddy at the thought that a potential pregnancy would have been welcome.

She arrived at work before Ruby for a change and began gathering the ingredients for the angel food donuts. Fortunately, Ruby had spent an hour after closing the day before cutting up strawberries for the compote, a task Maggie was happy not to have to undertake first thing in the morning.

By the time Ruby arrived, Maggie had already begun her first double batch of cinnamon roll dough and prepared two trays of angel food donuts for the display case. She was careful to set aside a half dozen just for Orson.

"Don't you think his days of overindulgence are over with after the mincemeat pie incident?" Ruby asked when she arrived.

"How well do you know Orson again?" Maggie said with an exaggerated eye roll. "We both know he's going to eat what he's going to eat regardless of how it affects him."

"Sometimes I wonder who's the parent and who's the child." Ruby hesitated and gazed at Maggie for a moment. "What happened last night?"

"What do you mean?" Maggie asked.

"From the time you left work yesterday to this morning, you've changed considerably," Ruby said. "You even look different. Your face isn't all screwed up in concern and worry."

"Thanks, I think," Maggie said. "We went out to dinner with Bradley, Suzan, and the kids last night in Joplin."

"That explains it. You got your mind off of Dessi's death."

"I guess you could say that." Maggie smiled. "How about you? You seem to be in a better place, too."

"I spent some time with the calves out in the pasture," Ruby said. "I guess it was the sheer physicality of the work that snapped me out of worry and concern."

"Whatever it takes I guess," Maggie said. "Don't get me wrong. I know a woman died, and I really hope they find out who did it."

"Me too," Ruby said. "I thought about Angel last night."

"So did I. Brett had a good point."

"And I'm sure you're going to share it with me," Ruby urged.

"Think about it," Maggie said. "If his friend Captain Flint had been tipped off about checking out the lady at the donut shop, that had to come from someone who knew of my very brief interaction with Angel and Dessi in the first place."

"Does he think it was Angel who said something?"

"It's kind of the only thing that makes sense."

"Based on that short timeline, I suppose so."

"I can't help but wonder where Angel is right now," Maggie said. "The sun is just coming up, let's go see if the food truck is still there."

"Lead the way."

Maggie hesitated long enough to grab a fresh cup of coffee for herself and Ruby. They walked through the front dining area, careful to avoid the tables and chairs as they found their way through the dimly lit room to the front door. "We could turn the light on, you know."

"But then people might mistake us for being open already."

Maggie unlocked the front door and stood outside on the sidewalk. She turned to her left and gazed at the large church parking lot. "It looks like the food truck is still there."

"I can't tell if the police tape is still around it."

"Ruby," Maggie said, turning slightly. She froze in place.

"What is it?" Ruby asked, gripping Maggie by the arm.

"Look," she said, indicating the parking lot in front of her.

Ruby turned and looked around, then shook her head. "I don't see anything."

"Exactly," Maggie said. She took a step off the sidewalk onto the parking lot and gestured toward the tall sign. "What is missing?"

"Oh, my gosh!" Ruby shouted. She followed Maggie into the parking lot. "Where is our food truck?"

"It's gone."

"Is there any reason for it to be somewhere else?" Ruby asked. "Think fast."

"Absolutely not," Maggie said. "Absolutely no reason at all." She headed straight for the front door.

"Where are you going?" Ruby asked, following her inside.

"To call Brett."

"What about the police?"

"I'll call Brett, you call Brooks." Maggie ran through the dining room and through the swinging door into the kitchen and headed straight for her office.

"Maybe we should look at the security footage from the cameras out front."

"There isn't time," Maggie said. "If someone took it, who knows where they're at by now. We can check after we call them."

Ruby said nothing else. Maggie picked up the phone and immediately dialed Brett at the Jefferson Street location. "What's going on?" he asked as soon as he picked up the phone.

"Did you stop by here and pick up the food truck?"

"The donut shop's truck?" Brett asked.

"What other food truck would I be asking you about?" Maggie snapped.

"What's gotten into you?"

"Nothing, I'm sorry," Maggie said, forcing herself to calm down. "Ruby and I just went out front and noticed that the food truck was gone. Unless you took it, there's no reason for it to be anywhere else. She's on the phone with Brooks right now to report it stolen."

"Have you checked the cameras?"

"I'm pulling up the footage now," Maggie said.

She fell silent for a moment. She double clicked on the icon for the camera system and reviewed the footage. "It won't show me a thing," she said, pushing her chair back from the desk.

"Are you saying the cameras were tampered with?"

"No. Apparently it was rather foggy last night," Maggie said. "The lens appears to have condensation on it, and I can't see anything across the parking lot."

"Nothing at all?" Brett sighed.

"Wait a minute." Maggie pulled her chair back to the desk and leaned forward, staring at the screen. "I think I see taillights, but nothing else."

"What time was it?"

Maggie clicked the mouse to stop the footage. "It looks like three twenty-three in the morning."

"I'll call you back," Brett said.

"Hang on a minute. Do you think this has anything to do with everything else that's been going on?"

"I can't be sure," Brett said. "But I plan to find out."

CHAPTER EIGHT

"And you're sure you didn't see anything when you arrived at work this morning?" Brooks asked Maggie. They were seated at a table close to the counter.

"No, I didn't see anything," Maggie confirmed. "As you know, I never drive through the parking lot when I arrive at work."

He nodded. "I've reviewed the security footage myself, and I'm afraid there isn't a lot to go on. The lens had too much condensation on it."

"Yeah, but, how easy can it be to hide a food truck?" Orson asked from the Old Timer's table. Maggie was grateful that the dining room was practically empty, aside from Orson.

"That's the point," Brooks said. "And hopefully that will aid us in recovering the food truck."

"Doesn't it strike you as odd that our food truck was stolen around the same time that a woman's body was discovered? I understand the two may not be connected, but the fact that she has a food truck makes me wonder."

"It's definitely curious," Brooks agreed. "I plan to look into this from all angles. I hope you understand that."

"Of course I do," Maggie said. "Thanks for coming out and talking to me in person."

"This is a bit of a high priority right now. I agree that it seems odd that the woman who was found out by the lake also had a food truck."

"Except for the fact that her food truck wasn't stolen," Maggie said.

"Still, the timing is odd." Brooks stood up and extended his hand to Maggie. "I'll be in touch as soon as I can."

"Thanks." Maggie stepped to the side and left room for Myra to have a brief conversation with her husband before they returned to their respective positions. Orson rose from his seat and joined her on the far end of the front counter.

"Who steals a food truck?" he asked, shaking his head.

"I guess if we knew the answer to that question, we might know who took mine."

"Yeah," Orson nodded. "I bet it was that one woman."

"Which one?"

"The one whose partner was killed."

"You think Angel Harris took my food truck? Why on earth would you think that?"

"Why not?" He shrugged. "Now that her partner is dead, she's probably not going to be able to keep the one she has."

"Orson," Maggie said. "We have no way to know if Angel even wants to stay in the food truck business."

"You remember what she said the other day, don't you?"

"About what, exactly?" Maggie asked.

"When she was in here, she said that her partner is the one who talked her into starting a food truck," Orson reminded her. "It sounds like this wasn't her original idea."

"You really hear everything that goes on around here, don't you?" Maggie shook her head. "And yes, to answer your question. Angel did say that she had a successful business in Tulsa before Dessi convinced her to open a food truck."

"Maybe it was really bad advice," Orson said. "Maybe Angel has lost everything thanks to Dessi's bad advice and now that Dessi is gone, Angel has nothing left. So, she took your food truck."

"But what about what you said a few minutes ago?" Maggie asked, reminding him of his words. "It isn't like you can steal a food truck and expect it to go unnoticed. And why steal someone else's food truck? Why not steal the one she already owns?"

"I don't know," Orson said. "I was just testing theories." He returned to his seat and sipped his coffee. Maggie shook her head again before making her way into the kitchen.

"What's the matter with you?" Ruby asked.

"Oh, you know Orson," Maggie said. "He's out there spouting theories about who took the food truck."

"I hope he didn't share them with Brooks."

"I'm surprised you didn't hear him from back here," Maggie said. "Sometimes that man doesn't know how to be quiet."

"So, what happened with Brooks?" Ruby asked.

She shrugged. "Nothing really. He said he'd be in touch."

"Why do I detect a bit of doubt in your voice?"

"I don't really doubt that Brooks will investigate," Maggie said. "I'm just fully aware of the fact that there's a murder investigation going on at the same time. And of course that takes priority. I would never expect it to be any other way."

"Unless," Ruby said slowly, drying her hands on a clean towel. "The theft of our food truck has something to do with the murder."

"Brooks hinted that he thinks it might," Maggie said. "I just don't see how. Why would someone steal a food truck after killing the owner of another food truck? I understand the timing is suspicious, but I don't see how the crimes are related."

A short time later, the lunch rush picked up and Maggie found herself busy and able to forget her concerns. Once in a while, though, she would glance outside and remember that the food truck had been taken.

Around noon, she retreated to her office. She picked up her phone and dialed Brett's number. He answered her on the third ring. "How are things going?" he asked.

"Typical," Maggie said. "Aside from the fact that our food truck is gone."

"I suppose that's a little hard to forget," Brett said ruefully.

"And the fact that I had to give Brooks a statement."

"How did that go?" Brett asked.

"About like you would think. He promised to make it as much of a priority as he could."

"You do realize that there is a murder investigation going on as well?"

Maggie swallowed the irritation she felt at his statement. "Yes, I realize that," she said calmly. "Brooks said he planned to look into the possibility that the two are related."

"How soon are you leaving?" Brett asked.

"Fairly soon," Maggie said. "Why? Are you coming home early?"

"No. I should be home at the normal time," he said. "I don't see any way to get away from here early today."

"Alright then, I'll see you at home."

"Hold on a second," Brett said. "Before you go, I think you should consider something."

"What's that?" Maggie asked. She closed her eyes and rubbed her forehead with her free hand, trying to prepare herself for another piece of bad news.

"There's a possibility Captain Flint may be around to speak with you now."

"Why would he want to speak with me now?" Maggie asked. "What's changed? I've been waiting to speak with him since Dessi's body was discovered, and no one has been around yet."

"The fact that your food truck was stolen sort of puts you back in the crosshairs of this investigation, don't you think? First the vague tip about the lady at the donut shop, and now this."

"Do you really think the state police are going to make it a priority to look into a stolen food truck?"

"Absolutely not," Brett said. "Unless it's somehow related to a recent murder."

"Maybe you're wrong."

"I hope I am, but that doesn't dismiss the possibility."

"I really hope they find the food truck," Maggie said. "And of course who killed Dessi."

"And I really hope it turns out that the two things aren't related."

CHAPTER NINE

After work, Maggie headed home, eager for a shower and a quick nap before Brett arrived. Following their phone call, she watched the front windows nervously for any sign of a member of the state police coming to question her about the food truck.

Instead of taking a nap, Maggie found herself burdened with restless energy. She busied herself in the kitchen, scrubbing out the sink, cleaning out the refrigerator, and bagging up the trash. She slipped her shoes on and headed out the back door to the trash barrel next to the garage. After she lifted the lid to set the bag inside, Maggie peeked around the corner. She was surprised to see a woman walking aimlessly around in the alley.

"Angel," Maggie said as the woman walked closer.

Angel stopped mid step in the middle of the alley and stared at her. "You. From the donut shop."

"What are you doing out here?" Maggie shivered slightly. "It's getting chilly, and it's supposed to rain. Why are you outside?"

As Angel walked closer, Maggie could see the redness on her tear-streaked face. Her hair was slightly disheveled. She shrugged and stared at the ground. "I don't know what to do."

"What to do about what?" Maggie asked carefully.

"I don't know what to do next," Angel said. "I was questioned by the police twice already I'm supposed to be there now for another interview, but I just don't know what to do."

"Why not talk to the police?" Maggie suggested. She reached around and felt the cell phone in her back pocket.

"This was all Dessi's idea," Angel said suddenly. "Coming here, buying the food truck, all of this was her."

"Angel, why aren't you speaking with the police?"

"I have nothing more to say to them," Angel said firmly. "I already told them everything I know. They've been through the food truck and questioned me about everything."

"Where are you staying?" Maggie asked.

"At the campground," Angel said. "By the lake."

"Why aren't you there now?" Maggie stepped back around the side of the garage momentarily. She was still visible to Angel but held her cell phone out to the side where Angel couldn't see it.

"What would I do there?" Angel asked. "Just sit around and wait for them to come for me?"

"Wait for who to come for you?" Maggie asked, trying to stall. She glanced to her left and tapped the icon for Brooks on her phone. She wondered if Angel could hear the phone ring.

"Wait for the police to come and arrest me," Angel said. "Or whoever hurt Dessi to come and get me next. I don't know that they're not coming for me, too."

"Hello? Is someone there?" Brooks asked on the other end of the phone. Maggie ignored him and continued speaking.

"Angel, why are you walking around in the alley behind my house?" Maggie said. "Were you aware this is where I lived?"

"What? No," Angel said, shaking her head. "Why would you think that?"

"You don't think it's a little ironic?" Maggie asked. "Forgive me for being suspicious, but my food truck was stolen last night."

"Wait a minute," Angel said. She focused on Maggie for the first time. "Your food truck was stolen last night? And you think I did it?"

"That's not what I said," Maggie said. "I'm just explaining why I'm a little suspicious about you being so close to my house."

"I didn't know you lived so close to the donut shop," Angel said. "How was I supposed to know that?"

"I don't know," Maggie said. "Why did Dessi approach me the way she did at the farmers market the other day? All I was doing was minding my own business and buying strawberries."

"That was just Dessi," Angel said wistfully. She shrugged her shoulders and stared off in the distance again. "She had a way of approaching people as if she was the center of attention. I've seen her do the same thing many times since I met her."

"How long did you know her?" Maggie asked.

"Not long," Angel said. "I already told you this the other day, didn't I?"

"I vaguely remember something," Maggie said. She was stalling for time. "You said you met Dessi in Tulsa? And she talked you into opening the food truck?"

"She talked me into shutting down my own business and investing in this food truck," Angel said. "For all the good it's done me."

"You don't seem to be very upset."

"Upset about what?"

"I don't know," Maggie said. "Maybe the fact that your business partner was just murdered."

"That was kind of a jerk thing to say. I think I better get going."

"Angel, wait," Maggie said. "Maybe I shouldn't have said that, but it is odd to me. I didn't ask for any of this, either."

"Yeah. I guess you sort of got roped into this, too," Angel said.

Maggie heard the crunch of tires on the gravel behind her. She looked back to see a police car pulling slowly into the alley. Angel gasped and glared at Maggie. Maggie looked past Angel and spotted another car pulling in behind her.

"What did you do?" Angel said.

"You need to go and speak with the police. Avoiding an interview is no way to prove yourself innocent."

"You really are something," Angel said, glaring at Maggie.

Maggie said nothing more but watched as one of Brooks's officers exited his vehicle and approached Angel. She turned away from the car, ready to head back inside her house. A tall figure approached from around the side of the house. His face was unfamiliar, though by his demeanor, Maggie was sure he was law enforcement. He was dressed in plain clothes, but pulled out a badge as he approached her.

"Are you Mrs. Mission?"

"Depends on who's asking," she said.

"Captain Andrew Flint, Missouri State Police. You are Brett's wife, right?"

"That's me," Maggie said, smiling weakly. "What can I do for you, Captain Flint?"

"I was at the Police Department when Chief Macklin received your phone call," he said. "Why did you decide to call and let him know where Angel was?"

"She told me she was skipping out on an interview," Maggie said. "I just thought it would be a good idea to let him know she was here."

"That's either very stupid, or very brave," Captain Flint said.

"Hey," Angel called out. Maggie turned to see her backing up several steps from the police officer. "You don't have to cuff me."

"I'm afraid it's standard procedure," the officer said, holding a pair of handcuffs.

"I can't believe you did this to me," Angel snapped at Maggie. "You're going to regret doing this."

"Hold on a minute," Captain Flint said. He walked around Maggie and approached Angel. "Did you just threaten this woman?"

"I'm not saying another word," Angel said, glaring at Maggie. She continued to stare as the officer fastened the handcuffs on her wrists. Maggie looked away as Angel was led to the back of the police car.

"This is insane," Maggie breathed after the squad carpooled back down the alley.

"Can we go inside?" Captain Flint asked.

"Sure," Maggie said. She replaced the lid on the trash barrel and headed toward the back door. "Brett will be home soon."

"Are you nervous about me being here without him?"

"Nervous? Not necessarily," Maggie said with a long sigh. "I'm just worn out. I don't know if that makes sense to you, but the last few days have been a bit much."

"Tell me about things," Captain Flint said, helping himself to a chair at the kitchen table. "When did you first run into Dessi Shroyer and Angel Harris?"

"A few days ago," Maggie said. "I was at the farmer's market and Dessi called me out for buying a bunch of strawberries."

"Was that odd to you?"

"Of course." Maggie nodded. "She was pretty rude about it, to be honest. We got into a discussion about why I had the strawberries, and they learned from that about where I work."

"And then Dessi showed up. Is that right?"

"Yes, as it turns out," Maggie said. She briefly related the encounter with Dessi for him.

"And then Angel showed up later that morning?"

"Yes, she was looking for Dessi."

"That's when we received a tip anonymously that we should look into you a bit more," Captain Flint said.

"That's what my husband told me," Maggie said. "He said you stopped in at the Jefferson Street location by mistake and recognized him."

"That is what happened." Captain Flint smiled. "Imagine me running into my old boss."

"And finding out that his wife was somehow wrapped up in this mess," Maggie said, chuckling softly.

"Something like that," Captain Flint said. "Tell me about your missing food truck."

"I'm sure you heard about the interaction between the pastor's wife and Angel," Maggie said. "My business partner Ruby and I were curious to know if Dessi's food truck was still parked in the church parking lot across the road. That's when we walked outside to take a look and discovered our food truck was missing."

"And here we are now," Captain Flint said. "And then oddly, Angel was walking down the alley behind your house."

"Basically, yes," Maggie said. "I can only imagine how that looks."

"Oh, don't worry about that," Captain Flint said. "It's clear you're just having a good run of very bad luck."

"I'm almost relieved to hear you say that. Believe me when I tell you Angel was the last person I expected to see."

"It makes sense that Angel would be sticking close by," he said. "After all, I think the vehicle we found Dessi's body in was the only car they had. Aside from that, there's the food truck, but we informed Angel not to remove it from the church parking lot pending the investigation."

"She said she had been staying at a spot out by the lake," Maggie said.

"She did? That's very interesting."

"Are you leaving?" Maggie asked when Captain Flint stood up from the table. "Brett should be here soon."

"That's fine. I'll catch up with him later," the captain said. "For now, I think I'm going to take a drive out to the lake. I want to have a look at her campsite."

Maggie walked him to the front door and watched as he pulled away in his unmarked vehicle. She sighed deeply, then turned around and collapsed on the couch.

"Maggie," Brett said. "Wake up. Can you hear me?"

Maggie sat upright and stretched her arms. "When did you get home?"

"Nearly two hours ago," Brett said. "You were passed out on the couch, so I decided to leave you be."

"Captain Flint was here," Maggie said.

"I know all about it." Brett took a seat next to her. "Andrew called me and filled me in on everything. Brooks called me, too."

"What a mess," Maggie said, shaking her head.

"You're taking the day off tomorrow," Brett announced.

"What? I already had a day off this week."

"And I've already spoken to Ruby. Don't argue with me about this, sweetheart. It's a done deal."

"I have to be at work tomorrow, Brett," Maggie said. "It's silly for me to take off another day."

"No, it isn't," he said. "This whole affair has you tied up in knots. Take the day off and get some rest."

"I'd rather be at work," Maggie said. "That way the day is filled with distractions."

"I think you'll manage," Brett said. "Just do me a favor and stay close to home."

CHAPTER TEN

Despite Brett's request that she spend the next day close to home, Maggie decided to head back out to the lake. After her last experience at the farmers market, she decided that she wanted to take her time perusing the various vendors' selections, this time without any interference from strangers.

After her first pass around the exterior of the market, Maggie carried two bags filled with vegetables and a bouquet of wildflowers, possibly the last of the season. She stopped for a cup of fresh apple cider and enjoyed the warm breeze, the first in several days.

An hour later, Maggie was ready to head back home with her purchases. She felt a bit more relaxed than she had since her first trip earlier in the week. She had even forgotten to check her cell phone for news about the murder investigation in more than half an hour. She was grateful her phone hadn't made any noise indicating messages or a missed phone call.

In the parking lot, Maggie loaded her purchases into the back of her car. She closed the trunk lid and stood up suddenly when someone tapped her on the back of her shoulder. She turned around, nearly crashing into Jean from the church. She took a step backward from the older woman.

"Hello," Jean said.

"Can I help you with something?" Maggie felt the muscles in her neck and shoulders tense immediately.

"I didn't mean to startle you."

"I'm sorry," Maggie said. She leaned against the back of the car. "I have had a few days of high anxiety this week."

"I imagine you have," Jean said. "I understand your food truck was stolen."

Maggie nodded her head slowly. "You didn't see anything, did you?"

"Me? No, I saw nothing," Jean said. "If I had, I would have gone straight to the police."

"I suppose you would have." Maggie gazed off in the distance toward the lake and exhaled slowly. "Of course you would have. I'm sorry again. It's been a very strange week."

"You're telling me," Jean said. "We haven't had so much excitement around here since the rummage sale last summer. Two of our regulars got in a fist fight over a basket of Tupperware." She leaned in close to share the gossip.

"I wish this anxiety was over Tupperware," Maggie said. "I'm worried about my food truck, of course. But a woman was murdered."

"I know," Jean said. "Our head deacon was questioned for hours about that situation."

"He's the one who confronted Angel, right? Rick was his name?"

"Rick Holcomb," Jean said, nodding. "His wife told me they kept him at the police station for more than four hours asking questions."

"Is he back home now?" Maggie asked.

"Yes, and ready to resign as head of the deacons," Jean said. "I can't say that I blame him."

"This has been quite a mess for all of you."

"I just hope they get it sorted out," Jean said. "I knew as soon as I saw that food truck there would be trouble. And it didn't take long to hear those two girls raising the roof at each other."

"You heard them fighting?" Maggie asked.

"They were fighting all right. Of course, they were behind closed doors, so to speak, in their food truck so I have no idea who said what."

"What did you overhear?"

"Basically, one of them shouting at the other for making her come to Missouri in the first place," Jean said. "The other one told her that she never forced her. They argued about business stuff. Money, closing businesses down, not affording what they're doing. It was a mess."

"It sure sounds that way," Maggie said.

"And then you heard the one the other day," Jean continued. "It sounds like she was brought here under false pretenses. I think that's how you say it."

"I think you mean Angel," Maggie said. "And yes, it sounds as if she was told a few tall tales about the property next to your church."

"I just hope she didn't kill that other girl. I mean, I know Rick didn't do it. I just hope they figure out who it was."

"So do I."

"What did the police say about your food truck?" Jean asked.

"Not much so far," Maggie said. "They've mainly just been asking me questions."

"Again, I hope they figure it out soon," Jean said. "It does seem a little ironic."

"That's what everyone has been saying," Maggie said. She was quickly tiring of the subject of the conversation and wanted to get home with her purchases.

"Well, listen," Jean said. "I'm sure you'll get your food truck back soon. We sure do like the fact that you're located right across the street from our church."

"I appreciate your business." Maggie smiled again and headed to her driver's side door.

"One more thing," Jean said, leaning into the door before Maggie closed it.

"What's that?" Maggie said patiently.

"You might ask Rick about your food truck," Jean suggested.

"Oh? What would he know about it?"

"He manages the church facilities," Jean said. "I'm not sure if there was anything on our security cameras or if it points over to your place, but if so, he would have seen it."

"Thanks for that tip," Maggie said, unsure if the police had been over to talk to him about it yet. "Do you know where I can find him?"

"He's at the church right now," Jean said. "He has a lot to catch up on after his day at the police station." She stepped back from the car and headed toward the farmer's market entrance.

When Maggie reached the side of town close to where her home and the donut shop were located, she decided to skip the side street that led to her house. Instead, she headed for the road that separated her donut shop from the church across the street. Jean had mentioned that Rick would be at the facility, and Maggie decided it was time for a quick chat with him.

As she passed the donut shop parking lot, her heart sank a little when her eyes landed on the empty parking spot where the food truck used to be.

Maggie parked on the opposite side of the church from the waffle truck, blocking it from her view. She spotted a dark gray pickup truck parked beneath a canopy.

When she began walking toward the church entrance, she was greeted by a gruff looking man dressed in denim overalls. He frowned at her when she approached him. "The church is closed today."

"Are you Rick Holcomb?" Maggie asked.

"I might be."

"I own that place," Maggie said, pointing in the direction of the donut shop.

The revelation had an immediate effect on the man. His gruff looked disappeared. He smiled warmly and nodded toward the donut shop. "I love that place," he said. "My wife and I come in every Sunday after church for a cinnamon roll and a coffee."

"I'm glad to hear it."

"What are you doing here?" Rick asked.

"I wanted to talk to you for a minute," Maggie said.

"What about? I can't give you any advice on making donuts."

"I have all the advice I need when it comes to making donuts." Maggie smiled. "I wanted to talk to you about the food truck over here." She gestured in the direction of the far side of the church.

"Oh, that nightmare," Rick said. He picked up a large trash bag at his feet and continue to carry it to an outdoor trash bin, fenced off from the rest of the parking lot. "There's not much to tell you about that. They never should have parked there in the first place."

"Were you here the night before last?" Maggie asked. "My own food truck went missing, and I wondered if you had seen anything."

"Your food truck," Rick said. The information appeared to be a complete surprise to him. "You know what? I didn't even look over there long enough to notice it missing."

"So, you didn't see anything?"

"Unfortunately, no. And we don't have any cameras looking in your direction," Rick said. "I spent most of the last couple days talking to half a dozen different people from three different law enforcement agencies. They were questioning me about that girl who died."

"Dessi Shroyer," Maggie said.

"Yeah, that's the one," Rick said. "I keep telling them I had nothing to do with it."

"I'm surprised they haven't picked me up for questioning."

"I don't think you're a suspect," Rick said. "Then again, none of those cops can get their act together long enough to get much done, anyway."

"What do you mean?" Maggie was familiar enough with the Dogwood Mountain Police Department and the Dogwood Mountain County Sheriff's Department to have seen both agencies in action. There never seemed to have been a problem before.

"I don't know what it is," Rick said. He dropped the trash bag into a metal dumpster and turned back to face her. "But the local cops have turned over part of their offices for the state police. Meanwhile, the sheriff's department has pulled other people in for interviews. It's like they haven't shared their notes yet or something. There was even some confusion about when Dessi's body was identified."

"What confusion?" Maggie asked. Her mind spun with the new information he was giving her.

"Oh, something about the sheriff's department handling the identification, meanwhile the local police wanted to be involved, but they were shut out." Rick shrugged. "Apparently, the state police had to come in and take over."

"When did all this take place?"

"The day before yesterday."

"It was her friend from Oklahoma who identified the body, right?" Maggie asked.

"Honestly, I'm not really sure. That's the way I heard it, but I think that was part of the confusion between the different police departments," Rick said with another shrug. "Anyway, is there anything else I can do for you? I have a big project waiting for me inside."

"I just wondered if you could tell me anything about Angel Harris."

"Who's Angel Harris?" Rick asked.

"The other owner of the food truck. The one who wasn't strangled to death."

"What do you want to know?" Rick asked. "I think she's shady as all get out. I mean, I think she's up to no good. I'm not saying she killed her friend, but they sure fought a lot."

"Can you tell me what they fought about?"

"About that food truck. One of them apparently told the other one lies about what was going on up here. I guess it's no wonder one of them wound up dead."

"Wow, why would you say that?" Maggie asked.

"Because they fought so much that food truck was rocking back and forth," Rick said bluntly. "I thought they were having a knock down drag out fight over there."

"So, you visited the food truck more than once, is that right?"

"Sure, I did," Rick said. "But I never laid a hand on those girls. I'm not that way. I just told them they needed to get out of the parking lot because they have no right to be here."

"I see they still haven't done that."

"Not yet," Rick said. "The whole police investigation thing has stalled that. I've seen the other one running around, the shorter girl. Is that Angel?"

"Probably," Maggie said. "Dessi was a lot taller. Have you seen anyone else?"

"Like who?" Rick asked.

"Like the friend who was supposed to have come here to identify the body," Maggie said. "I think her name was Yara."

"I haven't seen anyone else," Rick said. "Just that shorter girl running around with her pickup truck. Only, sometimes I'm not sure what color hair she has because it seems to change."

"Wait a minute," Maggie said. "Angel has a pickup?"

"Yeah, she drives a pickup," Rick said. "How else do you think they got that non-running food truck here?"

"When was the last time you saw it?"

"Oh, it's been awhile," Rick said. "At least a day or so. It's a pretty heavy-duty pickup. It had to be to pull that monstrosity." He jerked his thumb toward the direction of the food truck.

"Thanks for your time," Maggie said. "Come by this Sunday after church. I'll make sure the girls set aside extra-large cinnamon rolls for you and your wife."

"Thank you," Rick said brightly. "I won't turn that down."

CHAPTER ELEVEN

Once she was back home, Maggie did her best to involve herself in various projects. She picked up a blanket she had meant to crochet, but she set the project back down and headed to the kitchen. She opened the cabinet to the right of the sink and began to reorganize it. Halfway through, she lost interest and shoved everything back inside.

She walked down the hall toward the small bedroom they used as an office and peeked inside. Maggie glanced at her laptop but stepped out of the room and closed the door behind her. She opened the door again, dashed inside, pulled the charging cord free from the laptop and headed to the kitchen.

While the computer booted up, Maggie poured herself a cup of coffee. She opened the browser and began searching for restaurants in the Tulsa area. She narrowed her search to waffles but came up with a national chain. She refined her search and found only one locally owned place that was not part of a larger franchise. She picked up the phone next to the laptop on the table and dialed the number to the place.

"Packs of Stacks," a male voice answered. "Can I take your order?"

"Do you serve waffles?" Maggie asked. She almost covered her face in embarrassment from the question. It was the only thing she could come up with to ask.

"We serve pancakes and waffles, to go," he said. "Have you never been here before?"

"To tell you the truth, I don't even live in Tulsa," Maggie said. "I was wondering if you remember someone named Angel Harris. I think she used to own the place."

"Angel Harris? Can you hold for a second?"

Maggie could hear the muffled sound of the phone being passed to someone else, followed by a brief conversation she did not quite understand.

"This is Yara, manager of Packs of Stacks," a woman said a few moments later. "Did you call to ask about Angel Harris?"

"I did," Maggie said. She was stunned by the woman's name.

"Are you a cop or something? Because my general manager told me to direct any more inquiries from the police to our company attorney, Gerald Lancaster," Yara said.

"No, I'm not a cop," Maggie said quickly.

"Then I'm hanging up now," Yara said. "You're tying up the order line."

"No, wait," Maggie said quickly. "Please, this will only take a second."

"Fine," Yara said. "What can I do for you?"

"First, can you tell me if your last name is Scott?"

The line fell silent, though Maggie could hear the woman breathing. "Who is this?"

"My name is Maggie Mission, and I'll make this as brief as I can. I'm located in Dogwood Mountain, Missouri. Two women showed up here with a food truck a few days ago, and now one of them is dead. Her name was Dessi Shroyer."

"I'm aware of all of this," Yara said quietly. "Both of them worked here until a month ago."

"Didn't Angel own the place?"

"Angel? An owner? Not on your life." Yara laughed. "How do you know about us?"

"Well, someone told me you were a former business partner who was here in Missouri looking into Dessi."

"Me? I haven't been to Missouri in over two years," Yara said. "And I only went because my parents dragged me to Branson on vacation. And I don't even like country music."

"Okay," Maggie said slowly. "Have you been looking for Dessi? Did you maybe call the state police and tell them you were concerned about her?"

"The police? No," Yara said. "Look, I've been taking phone calls from a bunch of different people who claimed to be cops over the last few days. I didn't even know Dessi that well. She worked here for like two weeks before Angel and her quit on the same day."

"They both quit the same day?" Maggie asked.

"Yes, and I already told several people about this," Yara said. "Listen, I have to go."

"Wait, just one more question."

"One more," Yara said. "And then I'm going to hang up whether you want me to or not."

"Fair enough," Maggie said. "Can you just tell me if Dessi or Angel gave a reason for leaving? Why did they quit?"

"Dessi left because she believed everything Angel told her," Yara said. "Angel left because she was going to be fired anyway."

"Fired for what?"

"That's another question."

"Answer me and I will go away and leave you alone," Maggie promised.

"I shouldn't be telling you this, but I'm getting so sick of answering questions about that woman anyway," Yara said. "The only reason Angel was still working here was because my general manager Gerald and I were doing our best to find evidence to tie her to the money that came up missing over the last six months. Without evidence, there was nothing the police would do about it, but we both know it was her."

"How much money was missing?" Maggie asked, hopeful that Yara would not make good on her threat to simply hang up on her.

"Almost six thousand dollars," Yara said. "We didn't put it together at first, but someone skimmed it off a little every day. Angel was the only common factor with each theft we could trace."

"That's very interesting."

"I have to go and this time I mean it."

Before Maggie could thank her for her time, the call ended. She stared at the computer screen for a moment, then wiggled the mouse and erased her previous search. She entered the name of the woman Angel had insisted Dessi told her owned the land next to the church.

In less than a minute, Maggie confirmed that there were no real estate agents in the area named Margaret Chase. But she found out quickly that there was a prominent agent in Oklahoma City by the same name, who also had a satellite office in Tulsa.

Maggie swiped her keys off the counter and shoved her phone into her back pocket. A moment later, she pulled up behind the donut shop.

"Maggie," Ruby said as she walked in through the back door. "You're not supposed to be here. I have strict orders from Brett."

"I need to talk to you."

"You heard what she told you," Orson embarked from his stool next to the baker's table. "You're supposed to be home resting."

"This won't take long," she said, ignoring Orson's wagging finger.

"What's going on?" Ruby asked as they stepped into the walk-in cooler. It was larger than the office and more soundproof.

"Have you seen Brooks this morning?"

"No, but he's on his way over here," Ruby said. "He has to drop something off for Myra. Why?"

"Because when he gets here, the three of us need to have a conversation."

"About what?" Ruby asked. "I hope this has nothing to do with Dessi."

"It might have everything to do with her and who's responsible for her death."

"Tell me everything."

"Remember the concerned friend from back in Tulsa who was supposed to have contacted the cops about Dessi?"

"Yeah, Yara something." Ruby nodded. "What about her?"

"I just spoke with her. She manages a carry-out restaurant that specializes in pancakes and waffles."

"The same restaurant Angel owned when she was in Tulsa?" Ruby asked.

"The same one she and Dessi both met and worked at in Tulsa. Angel never owned it. In fact, she was about to be fired for theft."

"Wow."

"You're telling me." Maggie said.

Ruby turned and opened the cooler door slightly. "I think Brooks is here."

"Good," Maggie said. "I think it's time we have a conversation with him."

"Let me get this straight," Brooks said a few minutes later. "You think Yara Scott never came to this area in the first place?"

"Tell me something," Maggie said. "Have you ever met Angel yourself?"

"No, she worked with the state police and the sheriff's office. And it was my officers who picked her up from the alley behind your house. I never saw her myself," Brooks said. "Why?"

"Who handled the identification of Dessi's body?"

"Why do you ask?"

"Well, did an actual deputy of yours go with whomever it was that identified the body at the coroner's office?"

"I'd assume," Brooks said. "Hold on a minute and I'll find out." He stepped into her office with his phone pressed to his ear. A moment later, he returned, frowning.

"Is that a no?" Ruby asked. "Someone just showed up there and identified Dessi, is that right?"

"More or less," Brooks said. "Why is that significant?"

"Because you have three different agencies handling this case," Maggie said. "Think about it, Brooks. First, Dessi herself shows up here the morning she was killed. Then, Angel shows up a few hours later asking if we had seen her. In all that time, supposedly a friend from Tulsa was in the area looking for her and called and left a tip with the state police to investigate the lady at the donut shop."

"That sounds like a pretty accurate review of this case," Brooks said. "But I'm not sure where you're going with it."

"I don't think anyone from Tulsa ever showed up," Maggie said. "And I think it was Angel herself who called in that tip and went to identify the body."

"You think it was Angel who tried to frame us?" Ruby said.

"I'm not sure it was that she really was trying to frame us," Maggie said. "That's why her tip wasn't more specific. I think she was just trying to create confusion and throw everyone off."

"Maggie, I need you to think very carefully about what you're about to say," Brooks said. "Are you accusing Angel of killing Dessi?"

"Yes, I am," Maggie said, nodding her head firmly. "I talked to Rick Holcomb over at the church today, too. He told me he only ever saw Dessi and Angel hanging around the food truck. He also said he could hear them screaming at each other from time to time and that the food truck itself was moving as if they were having quite an argument."

"I don't think that proves anything," Ruby said.

"No, but it proves that Angel lied about a few things," Maggie said. "For one, she claimed not to have had a different vehicle, but Rick said she drove a truck and that's how they hauled the food truck around."

"Okay, but that just means she wasn't telling the truth," Brooks said.

"He also said he never knew what color hair Angel had," Maggie said. "What if that means she wore wigs or something to disguise herself? Also, the time-line doesn't fit. The time she claims Dessi went missing to when she showed up here looking for her, doesn't make sense. We saw Dessi that morning, less than three hours before Angel was here. It takes more than three hours to get here from Tulsa."

"And if your different police agencies haven't put it together yet, it's possible that Angel has gotten away with it up to this point," Ruby said.

"How am I supposed to prove this?" Brooks sighed.

"You can start by getting all the officers together to talk, and then you all go out for a ride to the campground at the lake," Maggie said. "I think you just might find our missing food truck there, too."

"You think Angel stole the food truck?" Ruby asked.

"If my theory is correct, she did," Maggie said. "I think she plans to leave her food truck behind and leave with the donut truck. She'll wind up in some other small town after she has gone through the food truck and changed it beyond recognition."

"But why would she do that?" Brooks asked.

"For the same reason she left Oklahoma," Maggie said. "I think she took the money from her previous employer and made-up the story about Dessi forcing her to leave her business behind to open the food truck. I also think she was the one who made up the story about the land next to the church. I think that's why she killed Dessi."

"Because Dessi figured it out?" Ruby said.

"Exactly," Maggie said, nodding. "I might be wrong, Brooks. I accept that. But I have a hunch that I'm right. I don't think Angel set out to kill her partner, but they probably got into another big fight, and she strangled her because Dessi probably threatened to tell the police about the money in Tulsa."

"You're thinking Dessi gave her an ultimatum?" Brooks asked.

"You never met Dessi," Maggie said. "She's the type of person who would have read the riot act to a grizzly bear. She didn't seem to be afraid of much, including confrontation."

CHAPTER TWELVE

"I think you need to change the name of these donuts," Orson said the following morning. He was seated at the Old Timer's table staring at the angel food donut on his plate. He pushed a piece around in the strawberry compote as he spoke.

"Why would we do that?" Ruby asked. She stood over him with her cup of coffee in her hand. Maggie was seated at their usual booth waiting for Ruby to return.

"Because, that Angel woman turned out to be a very bad person. I don't think you should keep the name. It might be bad luck."

"We got our food truck back," Maggie called out from the other side of the dining room. "That has to be good luck."

"That wasn't luck," Myra said from behind the counter. "And even Brooks said so last night. You solved the case. Don't tell him I said this, but with so many cooks in their kitchen, I don't know if they ever would have figured it out on their own."

"They would have," Ruby said, turning to walk back toward Maggie. "It sounded as if the right hand never knew what the left hand was doing, but they'd have gotten it eventually. Our Maggie was just faster."

"I'm sure you're right," Maggie said. "But I didn't have time to wait and find out."

"I know and Brooks feels awful," Myra said. "And you know him. He never talks about work at home."

"He was pretty upset," Orson said, polishing off the last bite. "I still think you should change the name."

"And what would you call them?" Ruby asked, humoring him.

"Orson's Bundles of Delights." Orson smiled proudly.

"That is a tragically wrong name," Maggie said.

"They are angel food donuts," Ruby said firmly. "With strawberry compote. That's what they will be called on the menu from now on."

"Have it your way." Orson shrugged.

"I'm curious," Ruby said, leaning over her cup of coffee. "What did Brett have to say about everything?"

"He had to tell me all the things I did that would have potentially put me in danger."

"Like what, opening your laptop and calling someone?" Ruby said. "He really worries about you. Maybe a little too much."

"I've been known to get myself into sticky situations," Maggie said. "But he even thought it was dangerous for me to stop by the church to talk to Rick Holcomb."

"You went to the farmers market yesterday, too," Ruby said.

"Yeah, it was the last day for this season," Maggie said. "I never expected to run into Jean there."

"And that's the reason why you went by the church, right?"

"Yes, that's right," Maggie said. "It was my talk with Rick that led me to search for the fictional restaurant Angel claimed she owned in Tulsa. I was just following the trail."

"That does it," Ruby said, clapping her hands together.

Maggie raised a brow.

"That explains why you're always finding yourself in hot water," Ruby said. "You simply have too much time on your hands. You can't take any more time off from work."

"I don't know about that," Maggie said. "I actually enjoyed my days off this week "

"I'm just saying what Brett is thinking," Ruby teased.

"I don't think he looks at it quite that way."

"Seriously, though," Ruby said. "Now that the food truck is back safe and sound, I think we ought to think about what good it's actually doing us by just sitting here."

"You think we should sell the food truck?" Maggie asked.

"No. I think we ought to find more ways to use it," Ruby said. "Like maybe at the farmer's market this coming spring when it reopens."

"But the market is open only two days a week."

"Which is the perfect amount of time for the two of us to spend away from here," Ruby said. "You go one day, and I'll go out there the other day."

"Instead of taking our days off?" Maggie said.

"In addition to our days off," Ruby said. "We'll be finished before noon, and that will give us each another half a day off each week."

"I have to talk to Brett about this," Maggie said doubtfully.

"We'll both talk to Brett about it," Ruby said. "As a matter of fact, I plan to make him believe that it was his idea in the first place."

Maggie laughed. "That might help."

"If he thinks he came up with it, he'll fight for it to make sure it gets done. Also, since it'll be his idea, he can go through the process of hiring a couple more part-time workers here to help out when we're gone," Ruby said. A wide smile spread across her face. "Let him interview and vet the new people, while you and I get to spend one morning a week out at the lake. It is a win-win situation."

"I knew there was a reason the two of us went into business together." Maggie smiled. "I love the idea."

"Good," Ruby said. "I'm glad. Because we just might find out that it will take both of us to run the food truck on those days it is out at the farmer's market."

"But you just said you want each of us to take one day," Maggie said. "Now you want the two of us to go out there together?"

"I think Brett might eventually see that as a necessity," Ruby said. "You know, between our days off and all."

"You're terrible."

"No, I'm just tired." Ruby grinned. "I'm ready for a little less time on my feet at this place every day. And if the two of us hang out at the food truck a couple of days a week, we won't be wearing out quite as fast."

"It sounds like your mind is on retirement," Maggie said.

"My mind is on scaling back a little bit." She smiled. "I'm not ready to be put out to pasture just yet."

***

If you enjoyed Glazed and Accused, check out the next book in the series, It Curd Be Murder, today!

AUTHOR'S NOTE

I'd love to hear your thoughts on my books, the storylines, and anything else that you'd like to comment on—reader feedback is very important to me. My contact information, along with some other helpful links, is listed on the next page. If you'd like to be on my list of "folks to contact" with updates, release and sales notifications, etc.… just shoot me an email and let me know. Thanks for reading!

Also…

… if you're looking for more great reads, Summer Prescott Books publishes several popular series by outstanding Cozy Mystery authors.

CONTACT SUMMER PRESCOTT BOOKS PUBLISHING

Blog and Book Catalog: http://summerprescottbooks.com

Email: summer.prescott.cozies@gmail.com

And...be sure to check out the Summer Prescott Cozy Mysteries fan page and Summer Prescott Books Publishing Page on Facebook – let's be friends!

To sign up for our fun and exciting newsletter, which will give you opportunities to win prizes and swag, enter contests, and be the first to know about New Releases, click here: http://summerprescottbooks.com

Made in United States
Cleveland, OH
29 April 2025

16511560R00081